GREYFRIARS BOBBY

Ruth Brown

RED FOX

"I'm fed up with sightseeing," moaned Tom. "It's too hot and I'm thirsty."

"Well, you're in luck," said Becky. "Here's a fountain. Have a drink."

"It's a drinking fountain for people *and* dogs," said Tom, reading the inscription.

A tribute to the affectionate fidelity of Greyfriar's Bobby. In 1858 this faithful dog followed the remains of his master to Greyfriar's Churchyard and lingered near the spot until his death in 1872.

GREYFRIARS BOBBY

For Fraser

A Red Fox Book

Published by Random House Children's Books
61-63 Uxbridge Road, London W5 5SA

A division of The Random House Group Ltd
London Melbourne Sydney Auckland
Johannesburg and agencies throughout the world

10

First published in Great Britain by
Andersen Press Ltd 1995
Red Fox edition 2000

Printed and bound in Hong Kong

THE RANDOM HOUSE GROUP Limited Reg. No. 954009
www.**kidsatrandomhouse**.co.uk

ISBN 978 0 099 72121 5
(from January 2007)
0 09 972121 X

"Let's go into the churchyard," said Tom.

GREY

"Do you think we would have seen Bobby the dog if we'd come in here a hundred years ago?"

"Of course you would," said the gardener. "He'd have been lying in the sun in this special place that was his home for the last years of his life.

Back then, you would have found him sound asleep, dreaming of the days before he lived in the churchyard. Those were the days when…

...Bobby used to help his master, Old Jock, guard the cattle which were brought into the city each evening for the market the following day.

The story goes that, in the mornings, after work, Jock and Bobby would visit the café owned by Mrs Ramsay, who would always save special titbits for Bobby—a bone, a bun or even a piece of pie.

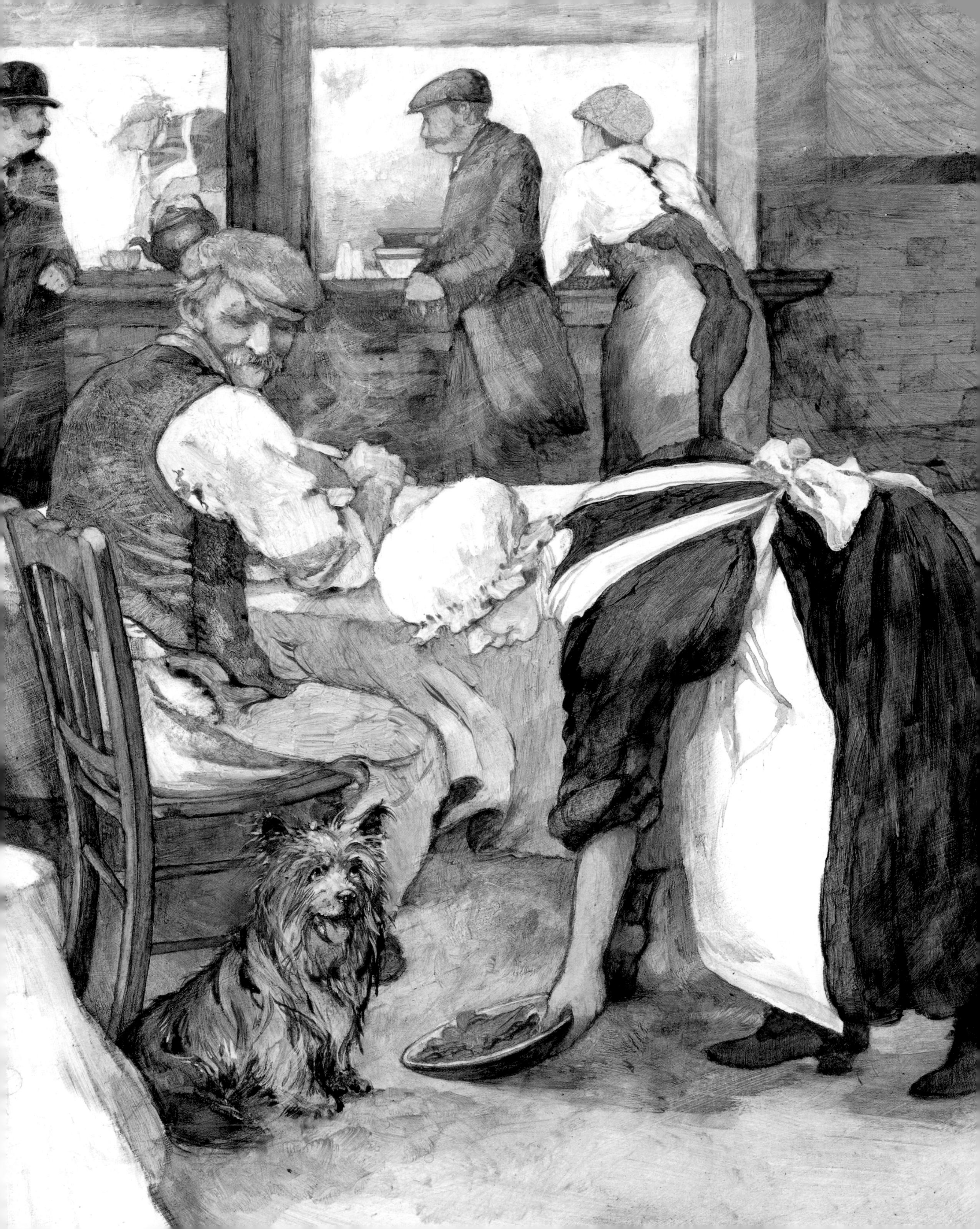

On their rare days off they'd walk for miles in the hills
where Old Jock had lived as a boy.

But in the winter they would stay in the city, still guarding the cattle despite the freezing winds and bitter cold that eventually made Old Jock so ill that he died.

And, on a grey morning, Bobby followed his master for the last time—to the churchyard of Greyfriars.

He got as close as he could to Old Jock and that's where he stayed. But how cold and hungry he was that night, huddled against the great, granite stones.

He remembered the café—if he went there by himself would there still be a bone, a bun or a piece of pie saved for him?

Of course there was—and when Mrs Ramsay found out where Bobby was living, there was food for him every day. The people were so touched by the loyalty of the little dog that they looked out for him and looked after him.

CAFE

He was given his own engraved collar, and water bowl, and, best of all, official permission to live in the churchyard—and that's where he stayed for fourteen years,

until, finally, he too was buried there—near his beloved master, Old Jock."

"What a story," said Becky.
"Aye," agreed the gardener. "Bobby never forgot his old friend."
"I don't think we'll ever forget Bobby," said Tom.